The HOME Team
Boston Bruins®

Written by Holly Preston
Illustrated by James Hearne

Always Books Ltd.

The Home Team: Boston Bruins®

Manufactured by Friesens Corporation in Altona, MB, Canada
November 2014
Job # 206296

Library and Archives Canada Cataloguing in Publication

Preston, Holly, author
The home team : Boston Bruins / written by Holly Preston ; illustrated by James Hearne.

ISBN 978-0-9869244-8-4 (pbk.)

1. Boston Bruins (Hockey team)—Juvenile fiction. I. Hearne, James, 1972-, illustrator II. Title.

PS8631.R467H64215 2014   jC813'.6   C2014-906583-3

Layout by Heather Nickel

MIX
Paper from
responsible sources
FSC® C016245

FSC
www.fsc.org

Always Books Ltd.
AFANFORLIFE.COM

For all young **BRUINS**® fans
who know there's no team like ours!

There was nothing better than playing hockey …

… except watching hockey when the **BOSTON BRUINS** played.

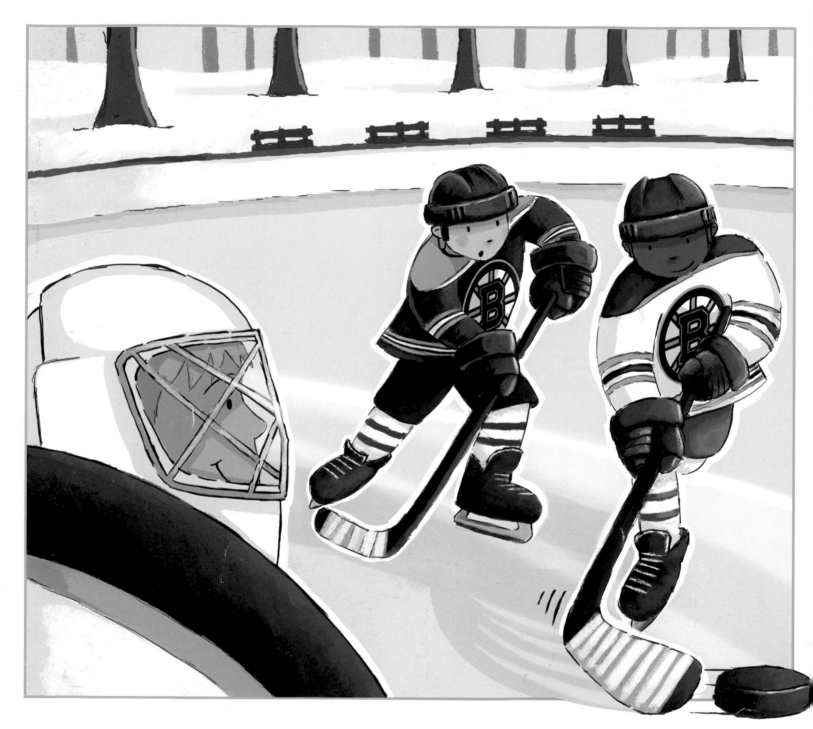

Mason played defense. Benjamin played forward. Brett was in goal.
The boys played different positions. They had the same dream:
to one day play for the **BOSTON BRUINS**.

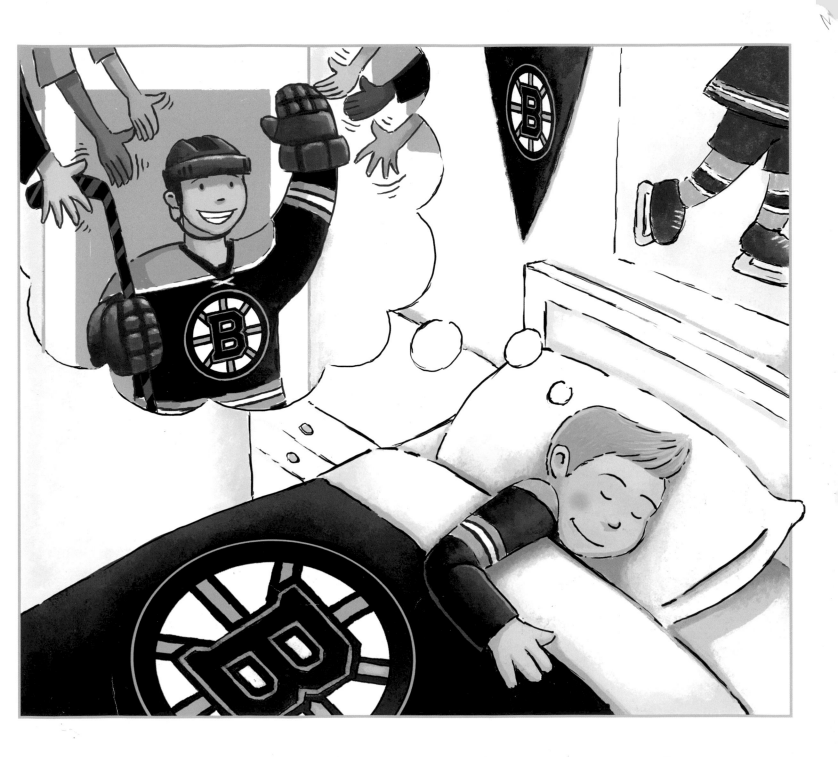

Even after playing all day, Benjamin dreamed only about hockey.

The only problem was Benjamin never scored. Ever.
The puck went high. The puck went low.
The puck went everywhere but where it was supposed to go.

How can I ever become one of the **BOSTON BRUINS**? Benjamin wondered.

His sister Emma was the best goal scorer in the neighborhood.

"The **BRUINS** were little boys once, too, Benjamin," his dad said.
"They didn't become hockey stars overnight.

His mom said, "You can learn a lot by watching what the **BRUINS** do."
She'd been a **BRUINS** fan forever.

The **BRUINS** are great skaters.

They make big plays.

They shoot. They score!

And make a million saves.

"The only way to get better is to practice," said Mason.
And so they practiced hard. And then came the best surprise they'd ever had.
"We're going to a **BRUINS** game!" Brett yelled.

But at the game, the **BRUINS'** top scorer wasn't scoring at all!
"Something is wrong," said Benjamin.

The next day on the way to the rink, Benjamin found a shiny chain.
He put it on and … he got a goal! And then another one!
"That's a good luck charm, for sure," Emma said.

"Our player lost his good luck charm, kids," said Dad. "Maybe *that's* why he hasn't been scoring." The children knew hockey players were superstitious. They also knew where that charm was …

And what they had to do next!

Benjamin seized the moment.
"What does it take to play for the **BOSTON BRUINS**?" he asked.

Play like a team…

...and with heart.

Never give up.

Believe in yourself.

"The **BRUINS** are the greatest team in the NHL," said Mason.

"We're going to be **BRUINS** fans forever," added Brett.

Everything was the way it should be.

All the next week Benjamin practiced and practiced.
He no longer had the good luck charm, but he had something else—
he believed in himself.

And that was all he really needed.

But Benjamin, like all hockey players, knew a little luck always helps…

…especially when you're playing for the Stanley Cup®!

ABOUT THE AUTHOR
Holly Preston

Holly Preston is a journalist who worked for CTV and CBC. She grew up watching NHL hockey with her brother and father. Now she creates children's picture books for professional sports teams. She hopes Bruins fans will enjoy having a book that celebrates their home team and encourages young fans to find a love of reading.

ABOUT THE ILLUSTRATOR
James Hearne

Born in London England, James began his art career at the tender age of eight, selling drawings to guests at his grandparents' hotel. He continues to sell his whimsical illustrations around the globe as a full-time illustrator and full-time hockey fan.